DEATH AT THE
VILLA TARCONTI

AN SAT VOCABULARY NOVELETTE

ERICA ABBETT

VOCABBETT

BIG WORDS MADE SIMPLE.

Death at the Villa Tarconti
Copyright © 2019 by Erica Abbett

For information about special discounts available for bulk purchases, sales promotions, fundraising and educational needs, contact Erica Abbett at contact@vocabbett.com.

Disclaimer in Legalese:
Individual results will vary. Vocabbett ("We") cannot guarantee success or improvement merely upon access, purchase, or completion of our products, services, courses, or other materials. Any results you see referenced here or elsewhere are not guaranteed or typical.

Disclaimer in plain English:
I'm going to do the very best I can to help you, but ultimately, the only person who can improve your vocabulary (and SAT/ACT score) is you. Please don't sue me.

AN INTRODUCTION TO
VOCABBETT

Think about the words you know.

For the most part, you didn't learn them through expensive tutors or study guides so thick you could beat someone over the head with them.

No, you learned these words by incidentally encountering them a bajillion times — often in story form.

At its core, that is the heart of Vocabbett: the (scientifically-backed) premise that one of the easiest ways to improve your vocabulary is to simply encounter big words more often, preferably in story form.

The problem is — facing a mountain of material to learn for the SAT and ACT — we change the rules on your brain, favoring brute force memorization strategies over the stories your brain knows and loves.

The result? Your brain usually fights back, making you bored, frustrated, or distracted.

With Vocabbett, my goal is for none of that to happen.

That's why I feed your brain the stories it was designed to consume, each one **packed with words** to help you come test day.

***

This book contains more than 80 designated vocabulary words.

For your convenience, definitions of lesser-known words are at the bottom of each page, as well as a glossary at the back of the book.

Last thing — because you're unlikely to see a word once and remember it for life, Vocabbett resources are meant to be consumed in bulk.

If you enjoy this one, check out the others at vocabbett.com/shop!

CONTENT WARNING

This story is a "cozy" mystery.

There is no graphic violence, but it is still a murder mystery, and there is some explicit language.

Consider yourself warned.

CHAPTER ONE

A small part of me wasn't at all saddened by Norm's death. He'd been a lecherous old man, and I'd only known the guy a few days. When he heard I was from Texas, his only reaction was to look me up and down, then ask if I'd ever been a cheerleader for the Cowboys.

"You've got the figure for it," he winked.

Gross.

Naturally, I kept these emotions to myself. I was alone in a foreign country, and the last thing I needed was for people to think I was some sort of sociopath.

And yet the circumstances of his death...well, I wouldn't wish them on anyone. Not even Norm.

I shivered, adjusting the scarf I'd draped over my shoulders.

Enough of this melancholia. I was seated on an impossibly

Lecherous - Creepy; showing excessive desire

Sociopath - Someone without a conscience

Melancholia - Gloom; sadness

comfortable, cream-colored couch, my feet discreetly propped atop a wooden coffee table, and a merry fire crackled in the stone fireplace to my left.

Outside the aging windows before me, the rolling hills of Tuscany stretched for miles. The only other edifice in sight was another aging villa, perched on one of the hills in the distance. It was early October — not too hot, not too cold — and the air was crisp and fresh.

Who could imagine that such unspeakable violence could occur somewhere so beautiful?

I snorted, immediately realizing what a foolish thought that was. The Romans were some of the most bloodthirsty people in history. These hills had seen plenty of violence, from ancient times through the Renaissance, the Italian independence movement through two world wars.

"Does something amuse you?" a sardonic voice to my right asked.

The speaker was a man slightly older than I, late twenties probably, with tousled brown hair that had started to turn golden in the Italian sun.

His dress was country casual — khakis and a white shirt opened at the collar, sleeves rolled to his elbows. I knew from our previous exchanges — all equally acrimonious — that he was British, and his name was Jack.

"Not at all," I replied. "Just...something in my throat."

I returned my attention to the leather-bound notebook in my lap. It wasn't as practical as my laptop, but it matched the

---

Discreetly - Not in an obvious way; unobtrusively

Edifice - A building (usually large and imposing)

Sardonic - Grimly mocking or cynical

Acrimonious - Angry; sharp

surroundings better. I hadn't written a word in an hour, though I was supposed to be penning a bestselling novel.

That's why we were here, by the way. It was a writing retreat, and I'd scrimped and saved for years to attend, saving dollar by dollar as a teaching assistant during the school year, waiting tables during the summer, even babysitting at night.

The trip still wiped out my paltry savings account, but I was here. In *Italy*. A land in which I have no ancestral roots, but that I've dreamed of since childhood.

"I'm going for a walk," I announced, though Jack and I were the only ones in the room. "Do you need anything?"

He stretched, shirt tightening across his admirable musculature. "I'll join you, if I may. None of us should be alone right now."

I narrowed my eyes. "What do you mean?"

"Come on, Lucy. Surely you've reasoned it out."

Jack closed his notebook, leaving a fountain pen in the crease, and rose to join me at the doorway.

I was certain he'd stopped speaking at that enigmatic point intentionally, hoping to provoke me into wild speculation about heaven knows what.

"*Au contraire*," I remarked flatly. "I have no idea what you're talking about."

Jack lowered his voice. "A knife in the ribs doesn't happen on accident. Norm was murdered, obviously."

"So the police, and everyone else, immediately concluded," I noted.

"But by whom, is the essential question?" Jack continued.

Paltry - Small or meager

Enigmatic - Mysterious; Difficult to understand

Speculation - Thinking; forming theories without firm evidence

"The police haven't yet caught the killer."

"It could've been anyone," I said with a sweeping hand. "A junkie — they have them in Italy too. A thief. Who knows?"

"On the grounds of the Villa Tarconti? Yes, I know what the police said — it was far from the house, at night. Anyone could've snuck in. But do you truly believe that?" His eyes bore directly into mine, absent of all the banter and sarcasm I'd already come to associate with him.

"What are you saying, Jack?" Once again I pulled my scarf closer.

"I am saying, my dear girl, that there is a killer in our midst."

Banter - The playful and friendly exchange of teasing remarks

CHAPTER TWO

"You can't be serious," I said. "How many million people live in this country, and you think the bad guy is on the retreat?"

"Let's not be sexist, now," Jack remarked in the same old mocking tone. "The killer could just as easily be a woman."

I rolled my eyes. "It's a figure of speech."

"I have a few theories," Jack continued briskly, "all of which eliminate the two of us from suspicion, which is why I'm confiding in you."

"How kind of you not to suspect me of murder," I said sweetly.

"That, and I'd hate to see you come to harm." He took a step closer to me, then paused as a creak in the hallway heralded an approaching visitor. "Let's keep this between us, for now," he murmured.

Any passerby could interpret that statement a number of ways, I realized.

Heralded - Announced

Damn the man. Landing an Italian boyfriend wasn't high on my list of priorities, but the prospect would be impossible if everyone assumed I was seeing Jack, and he kept murmuring sweet nothings like that.

"I'll walk by myself, thanks. If I happen to encounter the murderer, I'll be sure to let you know at dinner."

I slid neatly past him, trotting down the white, stone stairs and into the Italian countryside. I didn't know if he was watching or not. I didn't quite care.

* * *

A murderer in our writer's group, I scoffed, kicking a rock in the gravel path. *This guy.*

Whom did I suspect, I wondered? The gap year couple from Argentina, who alternated between sneaking off to make out under the cypress trees, and shooting each other resentful looks over our daily writing lessons?

No, Isabella and Fernando might have a volatile relationship, but they were harmless enough. I couldn't figure out what they were *doing* here, exactly — Isabella seemed to have only a passing interest in literature, and Fernando none at all, but why should that be a barrier when you've got buckets of money? They probably saw our retreat as a clever way to stay in an Italian castle before meeting their friends in Greece.

Hmmm. Mrs. Hobbes, the elderly spinster who was fond of poking people with her knitting needles when she felt they weren't paying close enough attention? That's probably why Fernando was shooting Isabella dirty looks in our meetings,

---

Scoffed - Said in a derisive or mocking way

Volatile - Liable to change unpredictably, often for the worse

incidentally...

There were ten of us. How could Jack have possibly considered each of the suspects and determined who was still under suspicion?

Ratiocination, and the fact that I was walking downhill, quickened my step. If I were to take Jack's wild claim seriously, who would I *actually* consider a suspect?

Sexism notwithstanding, I couldn't really see Isabella, Mrs. Hobbes, or the three Australian women (who came on the trip together, and had known each other for years) plunging a knife into Norm's ribs.

No, if the murderer was in our group, it was one of the men.

Not Fernando, obviously. I'd never even seen him speak with Norm. He avoided speaking with anyone but Isabella, as far as I could tell.

Ricardo was a different story. An Italian in his early 50's, he was the embodiment of an upper-class European male — perpetually tan, trim, wearing collared shirts with one too many buttons undone and shoes without socks.

Roughly the same age as Norm, the two had quickly forged an uneasy alliance in the forced intimacy of our retreat.

But after dinner the third night, something transpired that caused an explosive argument. They were in the garden, and I could hear them shouting at each other in two different languages from my second-story room.

Incidentally - Used when someone has something more to say on a subject

Ratiocination - Logical thinking

Embodiment - An idea or quality in bodily form

Perpetually - Never-ending; always

Forged - Created

Transpired - Happened

By the fourth — and last — night that Norm was with us, he and Ricardo were sitting at opposite ends of the table.

Naturally I'd passed this information on to the police, noting that yelling at someone does not necessarily make them a murderer.

"*Non te preocuppare, principessa*," the officer reassured me. "In Italy, shouting is common. When I left home this morning, my mother was shouting, my sister was shouting. It will not — as you say — prejudice the investigation."

Norm's body had been discovered the day before, just a few miles from the villa. The death of an American citizen on foreign soil was no light matter, and the local police force had already turned the matter over to the *carabinieri*.

The local officer before me had simply been sent here to save face — the same bureaucratic dance happened everywhere, it seemed. The police resented having their jurisdiction overruled, so they kept their hand in the pot, but they didn't really have the authority to run the investigation.

Belatedly, it struck me that I was now a few miles from the villa myself. *Why hadn't I inquired which trail had taken Norm to his death?*

Turning on my heel, I started back towards the Villa Tarconti. The sun had begun its descent, framing the castle in crepuscular tones of brilliant pink and orange.

The view was straight out of a film, but the sight didn't

Prejudice (v.) - Make biased without proper cause

Bureaucratic - Overly concerned with the procedure at the expense of common sense

Jurisdiction - The authority to interpret and apply the law

Belatedly - Later than should have been the case

Crepuscular - Relating to twilight

cheer me. It would set quickly now, and I didn't fancy walking home alone in the dark.

Just then, a figure emerged from the shadow of a tree.

"You should not be here," a low, accented voice said.

CHAPTER THREE

"Jesus, Ricardo, what are you *doing* here?" fear made my voice sound angry. Angry was good. Angry was better than afraid.

"I came to pay my respects. The *polizia* were everywhere yesterday, but now...it is more peaceful." Ricardo reached for my arm. "But it is too late for a young woman to be out alone. Come, I will take you back to the villa."

I instinctively pulled my arm away and did some rapid mental calculations — the type that every girl, unfortunately, has had to make. *Fight, flight, or hope that neither is actually necessary?*

A line from a book I read flashed through my mind — something along the lines of, "Most people are more worried about offending somebody than being murdered." Because of this, they don't fight or flee. The embarrassment they'd suffer if the

---

Instinctively - Without thinking; acting on impulse

guy was above-board is a greater deterrent than death.

Well, in this case, I was unlikely to win a fight, and flight was impossible. I was a petite woman and he was a full-grown man. I could hold him off for a while, but I wasn't confident I could win an outright altercation. And we were two, maybe three miles from the villa. I may be younger, but he was in fighting shape for his fifties.

Naturally, these thoughts flashed through my mind in far less time than it takes to recall them. I don't believe more than a moment passed before I gave him an innocuous smile and said, "Great, let me just text Jack to let him know we're on our way back."

I strode past him, typing, "*W/ Ric on w path*," then hit send before Ricardo caught up with me. When I put my phone away, I kept my hand in my purse, finger on the trigger of my pepper spray.

Ricardo didn't miss any of these actions. "Very sensible," he nodded in approval. "I am a man who you do not know. We are alone. There has been a tragedy."

I bit my lip, but didn't withdraw my hand. "You forgive me for taking precautions," I said.

"*Certo*. I only wish my daughter displayed such sense. Children these days..."

Ricardo began a familiar lamentation — reiterating the woes parents have sung for thousands of years — moaning about how lazy his children were, how much he'd done to give

---

Deterrent - Something that discourages someone from doing something

Altercation - Fight; noisy disagreement

Innocuous - Innocent

Lamentation - A dramatic, heartfelt complaint

Reiterating - Repeating

them the opportunities they were now squandering, etc.

I listened with one ear, my senses more attuned to his hands and any sudden movements they might make. Unfortunately, being Italian, his hands were always in motion. My arm jerked more than once, ready to spray the bastard.

I didn't take a proper breath until we entered the rickety fence surrounding the villa.

Squandering - Wasting

CHAPTER FOUR

"What is this?" Jack was sitting on the tile floor outside my room when I returned."W/ Ric on w path?" He stood up, dusting off his pants. "You know I'm not the jealous type, but isn't he a trifle old for you?"

I knew he was being sarcastic, but I took the bait. "Thanks to our little chat this afternoon, I scared myself half to death when I saw him creeping around the scene of the crime."

"The scene of the crime?" Jack's face went deadly serious. "And what were *you* doing at the scene of the crime?"

"I didn't *know* it was the scene of the crime until I got there. I just went for a walk. I didn't realize Norm had taken that path, too, when he was — that is, when he died."

Jack took a deep breath. "I'm flattered by your confidence in me, darling. Only a true genius could interpret this

---

Trifle - A little (Britishism)

cryptic series of abbreviations and come riding to the rescue. But perhaps we should come up with a slightly more specific way of alerting one another when danger is near?"

"There *was* no danger," I replied, attempting to unlock my door. "Your paranoia temporarily infected me, is all. Do you honestly think you know more than the police?"

The lock was stuck, as was its charming tendency. I threw my shoulder into the turn of the key, then shoved the door with my hip. It swung open, and Jack followed me inside.

"Do make yourself comfortable," I said.

"Thank you," Jack seated himself on the settee at the end of the bed. "I'll leave in a mo', but this really isn't the sort of conversation I want to have in a public hallway."

"For goodness sake, Jack, if you're so confident in your theory that one of us is the killer, why bring it to me? Take it to the police."

"I did. They...They didn't take it seriously." A flush spread across his tanned face. I couldn't tell whether it was from embarrassment or irritation.

I leaned against the fireplace opposite him, folding my arms. "Perhaps it's time I heard the theory that disqualifies either of us from being the killer, but leaves the other writers exposed."

"It's simple," Jack responded, palms turned up. "The murderer is a deranged novelist. You've heard of method acting?

Cryptic - Difficult to understand

Tendency - Habit

Deranged - Crazy

This person is method writing. They're using us to add verisimilitude to their next book. The novel will be hailed as 'chilling' and 'realistic' because the author watched — and caused — it all to happen."

"Uh-huh. And that disqualifies us why?"

"You are writing a comedy, and I'm writing non-fiction," Jack said. "I've also ruled out Fernando and Isabella for the simple reason that they aren't actually writing anything."

"I'd ruled them out too, but for different reasons. The biggest being, I don't believe the murderer is here. They're probably a thousand miles away by now, or at the very least in some alley in Rome, where there's safety in anonymity."

"How can you be so narrow-minded?" Jack demanded. "Just because the killer's motives aren't rational doesn't mean they don't apply. If the killer were rational, he wouldn't be a killer."

"I have to get changed for dinner, and so do you. Be gone with you, and I'll try to forget how irrational *you* sound."

Jack's jaw clenched. "Don't say I didn't warn you."

Verisimilitude - The appearance of being true or real

Anonymity - The state of being anonymous

CHAPTER FIVE

I didn't have time for more than a shower and a hasty wardrobe change before the bell chimed. Thankfully, my newfound tan meant I needed little makeup, and dresses always look moderately presentable.

I made my way down to the dining room, already redolent with the heavenly aroma of garlic and rosemary, when the owner of the Villa Tarconti unselfconsciously took my arm.

"*Madonna mia*, child!" she cried. "Don't let the Italians see you with wet hair. They'll faint with shock!"

Margaret was 85-years old, and had eschewed a quiet retirement in England in favor of her current life.

From what I heard, she'd single-handedly transformed the estate from a crumbling pile of bills to the thriving establish-

---

Hasty - Quick

Redolent - Smelling of

Eschewed - Deliberately avoided

ment it was today.

I tried smoothing my locks with my free hand. "Sorry...I didn't have time to dry it."

Margaret tsked. "Nothing to apologize for. Just a silly local superstition. They think you'll *die* if you go out with wet hair. So charming! Ah, George...If you'll excuse me, dear."

Margaret seamlessly transitioned from one guest to another, making sure each felt acknowledged and comfortable. She hand-selected each one, and loved nothing more than bringing a diverse group together.

Tonight's dinner was more formal than we'd grown accustomed to. It wasn't black-tie, but seats were assigned and the food would be served in courses, rather than the more relaxed family-style of the past week.

"I usually host a nice dinner before this," Margaret explained, "but due to the unpleasantness of the past few days...it seemed better to wait."

I smiled as one of the waiters offered me a glass of Pinot Grigio. They were all volunteers who stayed at the castle for free in exchange for their service.

I'd considered going that route, but decided to swallow the cost in exchange for more freedom and flexibility. The airlines would offer no such incentive, so I'd be spending a small fortune either way. Better to work on my novel once I arrived than to wash dishes.

The man who offered me the drink looked more like a wild man of the mountains than a waiter — his bushy beard blended with his curly hair, though the latter had been pulled into a

---

Incentive - Something that motivates a person to do something

discreet bun.

"Thanks," I smiled.

He smiled back, then ducked his head and went to serve the other guests.

Taking a delicate sip, I made my way toward the massive oak table where dinner would be served.

Renaissance paintings graced the pale walls, and wooden beams crisscrossed the ceiling overhead. The room was lit almost exclusively by candlelight, as would have been the case when the villa was constructed in the 16th century.

Casually circling the table, I looked for my name on one of the neat calligraphy place settings.

"Lucy," Ricardo said, now dressed in head-to-toe Armani. "Here you are! Next to me."

I gave him a tight-lipped smile. "Excellent. If you will excuse me…"

Not that I expected him to assassinate me before dinner. There was just something about the guy I didn't care for.

Knowing he'd be less likely to follow if I was engaged in conversation, I approached Elisa, Margaret's niece.

Petite, slender, and in her early 40's, her dark hair was cut in a severe bob à la Anna Wintour. Like her aunt, Elisa had an international upbringing and spoke English, Italian, French, and German with equal fluidity.

"I'm glad you're enjoying yourself," Elisa said disinterestedly. "They always do."

"Erm, yes, well," I said, trying to overlook her rudeness.

Discreet - Careful; without drawing attention

Fluidity - Smooth elegance or grace

"Are you and your aunt close?"

Elisa's eyes returned to me. "Margaret never had children, never re-married. She's too in love with this place. I wouldn't say we're close...but I *am* the closest family she has."

Her tone was proud, almost belligerent. As Pinot sloshed over the edge of her glass, I realized she'd also had more than a little to drink.

"Well, your aunt seems like an amazing woman. I'll let you get back to your, um..."

But she wasn't listening. I slinked back toward the table, where people were beginning to seat themselves.

My night was looking bleak already.

Belligerent - Hostile; agressive

Slinked - Moved quietly, unobtrusively

Bleak - Dreary; not encouraging

CHAPTER SIX

Elisa was poisoned at dinner.

There'd been plenty of opportunity. She drank heavily all night, and by the end of the second course, Margaret was sending her niece pained glances.

The rest of us politely overlooked her hiccups and bleary eyes, but sometime during dessert, she began coughing in a way that was impossible to ignore.

Elisa clutched her throat, rasping and banging on the table before George — an American doctor on the retreat — leaped up and performed the Heimlich maneuver. The rest of us watched in horrified silence as she continued coughing.

"Out of the way," George barked. "Out of the way!"

He laid Elisa's frail form on the floor, presumably because the table had too much on it. Then he took her pulse, looked at

---

Presumably - Probably

her pupils, and did other doctor-y things. Brow furrowed, he said, "Call 911, or whatever the number is here. Elisa has been poisoned."

Margaret's hand flew to her mouth. "George, are you..."

"Now!" he snapped. "Explanations later."

Margaret moved with surprising agility for a woman her age. The rest of us would've helped, but we had no idea whom to call or where the villa's phone was.

"The rest of you, *out*." George pointed at the door.

We cleared the room in silence. I caught Jack's eye as we entered the *salone*, and his eyes were more expressive than anything he could have said.

Being Jack, however, that didn't prevent him from speaking.

"Now do you believe me?" he whispered. "It's time for a council of war. Meet me in the gardens in half an hour."

I gave him a withering look. "If there's a murderer on the loose, why would we prowl the gardens in the middle of the night? Just come to my room when the pandemonium dies down."

"That is more sensible," he agreed. "But I didn't want you to think I was being presumptuous."

I rolled my eyes and made my way back to my room. Bumping the door with my hip, I threw on the lights, not stepping inside until I'd completed a thorough scan.

Furrowed - Wrinkled; grooved

Agility - The ability to move quickly and easily

Withering - Intense; scorching

Presumptuous - Going beyond what is permitted or appropriate

A queen bed graced one side of the room; a fireplace, which provided ambiance (and life-giving warmth, for most of the castle's history), the other. A large window overlooked the dark hills of Tuscany. All normal there, at least.

I tried not to look too closely at the antique paintings of lords and ladies. They were beautiful, but in my current mood, felt more like a *memento mori*. Their subjects had passed on, and before long, we would join them.

I shook my head, clearing the morbid thoughts, but still propped my door open with a chair before finishing my search of the room.

No one was hiding under the bed, in the closet, or behind the bathroom door. A full five minutes after entering, I deemed it safe to close the door and lose myself in thought.

A poisoning doesn't happen accidentally, and none of the explanations given for Norm's death applied to Elisa.

And I was no poison expert, but surely something that took hold that rapidly was administered recently?

I tore a page from my notebook and began making a list of suspects.

Unfortunately, it was rather a long list. *Anyone* could've slipped a vial of poison into Elisa's drink, from the volunteer waiters to the people sitting next to her — though the latter was unlikely. She was sitting next to Margaret and the doctor.

Ambiance - Mood; atmosphere

Memento Mori - A reminder of death

Morbid - Having to do with death or disease

Deemed - Considered in a certain way

A soft knock at the door interrupted my fruitless musings.

I opened the door and, wordlessly, Jack went to the settee at the foot of the bed. Then he took out his notebook and said very calmly, "The doctor is writing a murder mystery."

My jaw dropped. "Have you seen it? Does it involve a stabbing and a poisoning? How did you—"

"I will answer your questions methodically," Jack said. "I took the liberty of inquiring about the novels of our fellow retreat-goers this afternoon. It wasn't hard — everyone loves talking about their work."

"Were there any other murder mysteries?"

Jack shook his head. "Not *per se*. Some of the men are working on James Bond-type books, spy thrillers, but nothing that significantly parallels our case."

"But George's does?"

"Quite. Certain details are different, of course, but the first two deaths are identical."

"Is there another?"

"Mmmhmm. Next, the heroine and her love interest are buried alive."

"Jeese," I recoiled.

"Quite," Jack said. "I felt I should warn you in case you find yourself looking to explore any nearby tombs, or something of the like."

Fruitless - Unproductive; failing to produce desired results

Musings - Thoughts; reflections

Inquiring - Seeking information

Per se - Intrinsically; by or in itself

Recoiled - Sprang back in fear or disgust

"I'll restrain my archaeological impulses until this lunatic is behind bars," I assured him. "You're going to tell the police, aren't you?"

"First thing tomorrow morning. Until then, sleep tight. And bar the door."

Restrain - Hold back

CHAPTER SEVEN

"*Che terribile,*" the cook was muttering to herself when I came down for breakfast. I hadn't been able to sleep, and was the first one there.

"Are you OK, Silvia?" I asked. "Have you heard from the hospital?"

Silvia worked at the Villa Tarconti year-round. She was younger than Margaret — probably in her sixties, with frizzy gray hair and a full figure — but the two had become as close as sisters.

"They say Elisa will be OK, *grazie a Dio.* To think something so terrible could happen here, in the Villa Tarconti! *Madonna!*"

She was holding an enormous bowl in one arm, furiously whipping the batter.

I breathed a sigh of relief. "But she's OK, then? Thank God!"

"She will return this afternoon," Silvia agreed. "But poor Margaret...the stress, to have this happen, so soon after..."

She didn't need to specify. I knew she was referring to Norm, and nodded sympathetically.

"This place — all it does is create beauty!" Sylvia said. "To help the artists and writers, this is Margaret's passion. When she dies, she will leave the villa to a foundation, so the work can continue. I hoped that day was far away, but after this week..."

"Is there anything I can do to help?"

"You are kind, but no," Silvia put her bowl on the counter. "Go write. Do that, and give her a good day."

I obliged, returning to my manuscript with renewed vigor. I sat on a bench in the garden for a full six hours, scribbling furiously in my notebook.

I didn't expect to fall into a writing spell, but once it took hold, I had no desire to break it. New plot twists emerged, and more than once I chuckled at my own wit. I was so absorbed, I didn't even hear the bell chime for lunch.

Dusk was approaching by the time I looked up. To my surprise, I realized that the noises I'd been hearing were, in fact, my own stomach. I stood, uncomfortably rickety after so many hours on a bench, and stretched my arms overhead. Time to get changed for dinner.

I only hoped we could get through the day without another calamity.

* * *

Obliged - Did as someone desired

Vigor - Effort; energy; enthusiasm

Calamity - Disaster

"Elisa!" I said with genuine joy. "I'm so glad you're OK!"

"I am lucky to be alive," she said grimly.

She'd changed into olive green slacks and a white shirt, clearly making an effort to ameliorate her appearance. But she couldn't hide her pale face or the dark circles under her eyes.

We met in one of the massive stone hallways outside the kitchen. I'd come to see if I could sneak any food before dinner, and Elisa was leaving a chat with Silvia.

"Do you mind if I ask," I said cautiously, "did they figure out what happened to you?"

"Poison," Elisa rubbed her shoulders. "Lucy, I beg you take care. The idea that someone could be acting out their novel...it is too horrible to imagine."

"What...what makes you think someone is doing that?"

"It's obvious, isn't it? A bunch of deranged creatives writing scary stories...I'm only surprised one of them hasn't snapped before this."

I didn't mention that Jack had the same theory. Whether they were right or wrong, there was nothing I could do about it. The police had been informed.

"Is there anything I can do for you?" I asked. "You must be exhausted."

Relief flooded her face. "There is one thing, actually. Silvia just asked me to fetch some wine from the cellars, but it's so cold and musty down there..."

"Of course!" I said. "Just let me know what she wants."

"You're an angel. Can you grab three bottles of Chianti and

Ameliorate - Make better

27

three Pinot Grigio?"

"Done."

Elisa gave me directions to the cellars, and as I made my way down a creaky staircase and through a cobweb-infested hallway, I didn't blame her for not wanting to undertake the journey. I'd never been anywhere near this part of the villa before.

Eventually the air grew cold and clammy, and the lights began to flicker. Had I taken a wrong turn? There were hallways and corridors everywhere. Did someone really come all this way every day?

I decided that if I didn't see evidence of the cellar after turning the corner ahead, I'd head back and find someone who knew the way.

Turning, I saw a large, open door. The wine cellar? But shouldn't the door be closed, to keep it cool?

I slowly advanced and peeked inside. No wine.

I planned to turn around, but the decision was taken from me. Two hands shoved me forward, and I was so caught off guard, I stumbled face-first into the darkness, falling onto the jagged floor.

I scrambled to stand, but the door screamed shut behind me. The echo of the hinges, and sound of multiple locks turning, was the last thing I heard.

CHAPTER EIGHT

Calm. I told myself. *You must remain calm.*

I closed my eyes, then forced myself to concentrate on the darkest part of the room until my eyes adjusted to the dying light.

The only illumination came from a grimy window at the back of the room. It was less than a foot tall and maybe two feet wide. I didn't think I'd be able to wiggle through, even if it wasn't far out of reach, just below the ceiling.

I walked over to it nonetheless, raising my hand to measure how far away it was — maybe three feet above my outstretched fingers. I jumped, but came nowhere near clasping the edge.

I turned my back to the window and examined the rest of my surroundings. The room was a small square — maybe 15 feet by the same. The floor and walls were stone, slimy with age. There was no food, furniture, or anything that could be

---

Illumination - Light

used as a weapon.

I sat on the floor, cross-legged, and put my fists to my eyes. Surely someone would notice if I didn't come to dinner?

But then, I'd missed lunch, too. Plenty of people had seen me working in the garden, morning and afternoon.

Whoever locked me in here would simply put out word that I was too engrossed in my book to be bothered. Writers are famous for their absent-minded tendencies. No one would think twice, and if they did, they'd just assume I brought food to my room.

The fact that I missed lunch reminded me of how hungry I was. Jumping up and down below the window would only tire me out faster. No, what I needed to do now was think.

Who locked me in here? I was pretty sure, now, that I knew.

* * *

The "unhinged author re-enacting their book" theory was just a ruse.

If Jack reported his suspicions to the police this morning, the doctor would be under surveillance by now. He wouldn't have been able to follow me down here and lock me in. He didn't even know I was going to the cellars.

If Jack reported him. The theory had been Jack's first, after all...

Engrossed - Entirely absorbed by

Tendencies - Habits

Ruse - Trick

No. I rejected the tempting, tangential argument. The killer wasn't Jack, or the doctor. It was the only person who knew where I'd be at this particular moment.

Elisa.

Things had happened so fast, and I'd been so confused by the "crazy creatives" theory, that I'd overlooked a motive as old as time: greed.

To be fair to myself, I couldn't have put it together before my talk with the cook this morning. But if Elisa was avaricious enough to think she should inherit the Villa Tarconti, and Margaret planned to donate it to some nonprofit, she might take drastic measures.

Like poisoning her aunt's mission?

If Elisa turned the retreat into something so twisted, so dark, that Margaret shuddered at the memory, she might reconsider her desire to see the retreats continue.

Two "accidents" hadn't been enough to give weight to the theory, but if all went according to plan — if I was found buried alive, or close to it — the "evidence" would be inescapable. Margaret would forever associate her work with the deaths of at least two people.

Elisa probably hatched the plan months ago. In our applications, we had to submit a synopsis and excerpt of our work. I'm sure Margaret — being of an older generation — printed everything out. There was no reason for her to keep the documents under lock and key.

From there, all Elisa had to do was find the murder mystery

Tangential - Related; diverging from the previous line

Avaricious - Greedy

— there was bound to be one in a group of ten novels — and consider how to re-enact it. Her aunt's pride and joy would be destroyed, and any thought of the Villa Tarconti being donated so the mission could continue would go up in smoke.

I clenched my jaw. What a *horrible* person she was. Elisa's plan wouldn't just devastate Margaret. It would poison her life's work.

The final kicker, though, was that she gave me faulty directions to the wine cellar. The only one who knew where I was going, she guided me into a trap of her own devising.

At the rattle of chains, I leaped to my feet. The sun had nearly completed its descent, but I remembered where the door was, and intended to charge it when it opened.

Elisa might be armed, but it was a risk I had to take. The creak of the door announced its opening, and, flexing my fingers, I sprang.

Gratified to encounter a body, I punched and shoved, but it wasn't Elisa's frail form under my fists. The figure was that of a man. Even with no light, the difference was unmistakable.

So I was wrong. At the moment, I didn't much care. I just had to get past him.

The man shoved me back, and when I landed on my backside, I gasped. *The door was shutting!* The sound was unmistakable.

I jumped up again, but the man was still in the room.

"Who are you?" I demanded, trying to get a closer look in the darkness.

Devising - Planning; creating

Frail - Weak and delicate

"Lucy?" a voice said in genuine shock.

"Of course it's Lucy, you psychopath!" I spat. "Who the f*** are you?"

But I already knew. The voice was cultured, British. It was Jack.

CHAPTER NINE

"So," I said. "All this concern for my well-being was just a ploy. What's your motive?"

I could tell Jack was trying to control his temper. "My *motive*? You silly twit, I was looking for you. I went to check on you before dinner, but you were nowhere to be found. I ran into Elisa..."

My voice caught. "And let me guess, she asked you for help with something?"

"How did you know?"

"Why do you think I'm down here? Damn our kind hearts."

Jack was silent a moment. When he spoke, he sounded a little queasy. "The heroine and her love interest, buried alive... But...it's the next set of deaths in George's book."

I paused for a minute. "Have a seat, Jack."

I explained Elisa's twisted motives, how she was using

Ploy - A cunning plan; scheme

George's story to poison the nature of the retreat.

"It's an awfully convoluted plan," Jack said, kicking a stray pebble.

"She has an awfully large motive: the Villa Tarconti."

Jack and I were seated in the dark near the door. Neither of us had moved, since by now, we couldn't see anything. The only hint of light came from the stars outside the grimy window. They faintly illuminated the aperture, but nothing else.

"Why us, I wonder?" I said eventually. "Wouldn't Fernando and Isabella be a better pick for the imprisoned lovers? Not that I'd rather it be them..."

"I suppose it was partially a matter of convenience," Jack sighed. "You and I were both available."

"Hmph. Well, I don't intend to starve to death down here. I don't suppose you brought any food or a flashlight?"

"Fresh out, I'm afraid."

"Figured. I saw this place when there was still some light. It's solid stone, Jack. There's no way we're *Count of Monte Cristo*-ing our way out of here. It would take a sledgehammer to move one of these boulders."

"The window, then?"

"It's our only shot. I *might* be able to squeeze through, if I sit on your shoulders."

Jack didn't respond immediately. "She's been planning this for months. Why lock us in a room with a window?"

"I doubt most people could fit through it. I'm not even sure I can, and I'm only 5 feet tall."

Convoluted - Extremely complex and difficult to follow

Aperture - Opening

Jack rubbed the back of his neck. "We'll only have one chance. If you fall on these stones, a concussion will be the least of your problems. There's nothing I can do if you crack your head open."

"What a comforting thought," I said, groping for him. "Alright, on your knees. I'm going to climb on your shoulders."

Jack obliged, then lifted me with minimal effort. Thank God I was here with someone strong, at least.

As he walked carefully to the window, I wondered if Fernando could even lift Isabella. I was pretty sure he'd been smoking since he was twelve, and I doubted there was much muscle under his graphic T's.

Better Jack and me in here than the two of them. We stood a chance, at least.

I shared this thought with Jack, and he snorted. "Don't count your blessings yet. We're a long way from safe."

"Jack, has it occurred to you that you won't be able to come with me? What if I run into Elisa on my way to get help? She killed Norm. I'm not saying I can't put up a good fight, but...that b***h is crazy."

"Norm wasn't expecting anything," Jack said. "You'll be on red-alert. Now, time to climb."

I hoped to find a latch, but the window was solid glass. I refused to be deterred.

"Cover your eyes," I said.

I carefully pulled my scarf from my neck, then wrapped it around my arm punched a hole through the glass. Old and

---

Obliged - Did (something) as someone asked or desired

Deterred - Discouraged

thick, it shattered in large chunks. I moved my arm around until there were no ragged shards left, wincing as one of the pieces slid under the scarf and nicked me.

"Done," I threw the scarf to the corner of the room. "But..."

I eyed the aperture once more. *How on earth was I supposed to get through this?* There was nothing to hold on to, and I'd need to be much higher up to slither out head-first.

"I'm going to have to crouch on your shoulders," I said. "I can't pull myself through like this, with just my arm strength."

"Whatever you need," Jack said. "Just be careful."

He wobbled slightly as I scrambled around, but thankfully we were near a wall. He rested his hands on it for balance, and I gripped the windowsill for dear life as I positioned my feet on his shoulders.

After a terrifying near-slip, I pushed my head and arms through.

"Almost there!" I cried, wiggling my bottom. Jack grabbed one of my flailing legs and gave it an extra push.

Scratched, but alive, I made it out.

"Oh Lucy," Elisa was seated cross-legged on a bench facing our window. "I wish you'd taken my advice. I *did* warn you to look out for yourself."

The knife she held glinted in the moonlight.

Aperture - Opening

CHAPTER TEN

I didn't bother trying to fight her. She had a knife, for God's sake. Instead, I ran.

I'd emerged in the gardens, a five-minute walk from the door to the *salone*. After dinner, I was certain people would be there. The door might be locked, but they'd hear me banging...

I didn't want to consider the alternative. Elisa wasn't far behind me. I could hear her footsteps crunching in the gravel, her breath ragged as she tried to close the distance between our sprinting forms. *Would I even have time to open the door, let alone bang and shout for help?*

Terror lent strength to my exhausted limbs. I skidded on a patch of rock and was certain I'd fall to my death, but somehow found my balance and kept running.

So close... "HELP!" I screamed. "HEEEEELPPPP!!!!!!! FIRE! MASSIVE FIRE!!!!! GET OUT OF THE HOUSE!!!!!!!!!!"

Emerged - Came out of (something) and into view

I kept screaming as I ran. Elisa wouldn't act with witnesses nearby, and hopefully they'd respond quicker to my pre-emptive howling than they would to me banging on the door when I got there.

All of my senses were heightened. I could see the door now with hawk-like clarity. I knew it swung inwards, and my arm was outstretched, ready to open it. That would be the riskiest moment, for I'd have to slow down, giving Elisa a chance to catch up with me.

I almost cried with relief when I saw the door move, silhouetting Margaret's slender form against the light.

"MARGARET!" I screamed. "KEEP THE DOOR OPEN BUT GET OUT OF THE WAY!!! ELISA HAS GONE CRAZY!"

Margaret looked alarmed, then horrified. Watching her face, I could see the exact moment when her eyes landed on Elisa, chasing me with a knife.

Margaret stepped aside, and I didn't stop running until I'd crossed the threshold, safe in the arms of the Villa Tarconti.

I needn't have bothered. Elisa's footsteps halted the moment Margaret laid eyes on her.

The jig was up. Elisa was caught.

* * *

"I cannot say how sorry I am to have put you through this, my dear," Margaret said for the 100th time.

Pre-emptive - Happening before something else, usually to prevent another thing from happening

Threshold - The bottom of a doorway; a point that must be exceeded for something to happen

39

It was a few days after Jack and I were immured in the cellars. Elisa had been taken into custody that night.

The next few days were a blur of police officers, interviews, official statements, and unusually long naps.

It was done, though. Our part was done, at any rate.

When the dust began to settle, Margaret invited Jack and me to a private lunch in her quarters. She had an entire wing to herself, and one of the rooms boasted a small table near a large window. I could hear the birds chirping on the rolling hills outside, leaves rustling pleasantly in the wind.

"Margaret, you won't let this affect you, right? I mean, of course it will *affect y*ou," I stumbled, "but you won't let it spoil your happiness, your life's work? That's what Elisa wanted."

"What she wanted was my money," Margaret retorted with unusual cynicism, placing down her tea cup. "But I take your meaning. No, the Villa Tarconti, helping people like you, it is my passion. Elisa cannot take that from me."

"Good," Jack said. "Because I can assure you, Lucy and I are just fine. We'll look back at this as a crazy adventure. A riot."

He was overstating it a little bit, but I supposed he hadn't been chased through the gardens by a homicidal maniac.

I would be fine though. My biggest injury were some scratches on my arms. Nothing more than a kid gets falling off a bike.

"Still," Margaret said. "You both worked so hard to be here...It is only right that I extend your stay, free of charge. Do you have any plans the rest of the summer?"

Immured - Confined against a person's will

Retorted - Responded in a sharp or witty manner

My jaw dropped. "Are you serious?"

"Of course! It is the least I can do!"

"I don't have to be back at school until August, and I'd quit my job before turning down an opportunity like this."

Jack smiled. "I'll make it work. Thank you, Margaret. You are most gracious."

We finished lunch, and Jack and I left together. We hadn't spoken privately since that night, and the air hung heavy between us.

Unconsciously, we made our way back to the drawing room, where a million years ago he first warned me that something was amiss.

Jack sat next to me on the cream couch, a feeling of contentment settling over me as we leaned back and admired the view.

"You know I was terrified, right?" he said finally. "When I heard Elisa chasing you, I felt so helpless...I'd have given anything to change places with you."

"I can imagine," I said. "But we're OK now. Like you said, this will just be a crazy story in a few years."

"What if..." Jack put his arm around me. "It was just the beginning of the story?"

I turned to look at him. "The two love interests from George's book, finding happiness in Italy instead of being buried alive?"

Suddenly serious, he said, "You know I'm mad about you, Lucy. I have been since day one. You're so stubborn, and there

---

Amiss - Wrong

Contentment - Happiness

is no one I'd rather be locked in a cellar with..."

I let out a laugh, and we slowly leaned closer to one another. Our lips met with an intensity that released all the emotion of the past week. Nothing else mattered.

"To new beginnings," I murmured.

ALSO BY ERICA ABBETT

Ahead of Her Time: An SAT Vocabulary Novel

Hera and the Headmaster (A Short Story)

Casting Call: Author Seeking New Villain (A Short Story)

Master Your Mindset (An SAT Prep Course)

The Etymology Course (An SAT Prep Course)

GLOSSARY OF TERMS

*When there are multiple definitions of a word, the definition
provided matches the context of the sentence.*

1. Acrimonious - Angry; sharp
2. Agility - The ability to move quickly and easily
3. Altercation - A fight; a noisy disagreement
4. Ambiance - Mood; atmosphere
5. Ameliorate - Make better
6. Amiss - Wrong
7. Anonymity - The state of being anonymous
8. Aperture - Opening
9. Avaricious - Greedy
10. Banter - The playful and friendly exchange of teasing remarks
11. Belatedly - Later than should have been the case
12. Belligerent - Hostile; agressive
13. Bleak - Dreary; not encouraging
14. Bureaucratic - Overly concerned with the procedure at the expense of common sense
15. Calamity - Disaster
16. Contentment - Happiness
17. Convoluted - Extremely complex and difficult to follow
18. Crepuscular - Relating to twilight
19. Cryptic - Difficult to understand
20. Deemed - Considered in a certain way
21. Deranged - Crazy
22. Deterred - Discouraged
23. Deterrent - Something that discourages someone from doing something

24. Devising - Planning; creating
25. Discreet - Careful; without drawing attention
26. Edifice - A building (usually large and imposing)
27. Embodiment - An idea or quality in bodily form
28. Emerged - Came out of something and into view
29. Engrossed - Entirely absorbed by
30. Enigmatic - Mysterious; Difficult to understand
31. Eschewed - Deliberately avoided
32. Fluidity - Smooth elegance or grace
33. Forged - Created
34. Frail - Weak and delicate
35. Fruitless - Unproductive; failing to produce desired results
36. Furrowed - Wrinkled; grooved
37. Hasty - Quick
38. Heralded - Announced
39. Illumination - Light
40. Immured - Confined against a person's will
41. Incentive - Something that motivates a person to do something
42. Incidentally - Used when someone has something more to say on a subject
43. Innocuous - Innocent
44. Inquire - Ask about
45. Instinctively - Without thinking; acting on impulse
46. Jurisdiction - The authority to interpret and apply the law
47. Lamentation - A dramatic, heartfelt complaint
48. Lecherous - Creepy; showing excessive desire
49. Melancholia - Gloom; sadness

50. *Memento Mori* - A reminder of death
51. Morbid - Having to do with death or disease
52. Musings - Thoughts; reflections
53. Obliged - Did as someone desired
54. Paltry - Small or meager
55. Pandemonium - Wild disorder or confusion
56. *Per se* - Intrinsically; by or in itself
57. Perched - Situated above something else
58. Perpetually - Never-ending; always
59. Ploy - A cunning plan; scheme
60. Precautions - A measure taken in advance to secure better results
61. Pre-emptive - Happening before something else, usually to try to prevent that other thing from happening
62. Prejudice (v.) - Make biased without proper cause
63. Presumably - Probably
64. Presumptuous - Not observing the limits of what's appropriate; assuming you can do things you probably shouldn't
65. Ratiocination - Logical thinking
66. Recoiled - Sprang back in fear or disgust
67. Redolent - Smelling of
68. Reiterating - Repeating
69. Restrain - Hold back
70. Retort - Respond in a sharp, angry, or witty manner
71. Ruse - Trick
72. Sardonic - Grimly mocking or cynical
73. Scoffed - Said in a derisive or mocking way
74. Slink - Move unobtrusively or furtively
75. Sociopath - Someone without a conscience

76. Speculation - Thinking; forming theories without firm evidence

77. Squandering - Wasting

78. Tangential - Related; diverging from the previous line

79. Tendencies - Habits

80. Threshold - The bottom of a doorway, but often used to symbolize something more important

81. Transpired - Happened

82. Trifle (n.) - A little

83. Verisimilitude - The appearance of being true

84. Vigor - Effort; energy; enthusiasm

85. Volatile - Liable to change unpredictably, often for the worse

86. Withering - Intense; scorching

Made in the USA
Las Vegas, NV
16 September 2021